I Can Squash Elephants!

A MASAI TALE ABOUT MONSTERS

Malcolm Carrick

The Viking Press   *New York*

First Edition
Copyright © Malcolm Carrick, 1978. All rights reserved.
First published in 1978 by The Viking Press, 625 Madison Avenue, New York, N.Y. 10022.
Published simultaneously in Canada by Penguin Books Canada Limited
Printed in U.S.A.
1 2 3 4 5 82 81 80 79 78

Library of Congress Cataloging in Publication Data
Carrick, Malcolm.   I can squash elephants!
Summary: A caterpillar in a cave has all the
animals outside terrorized by his echoing voice.
[1. Animals—Fiction] I. Title.
PZ7.C23452Iae   [E]   77-3455 ISBN 0–670–38983–8

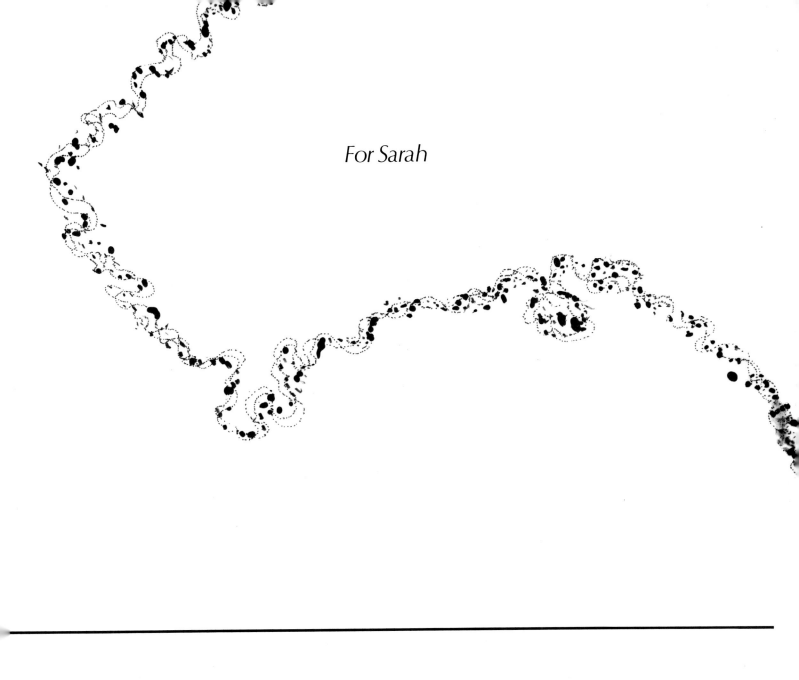

For Sarah

One day when Hare returned to his cave in the jungle, he found strange tracks leading into it.

"Who's there?" he called. "Who's in Hare's house?"

"It's only me," answered small hairy Caterpillar, who was inside sheltering from the rain. But his voice echoed around the walls of the cave and sounded loud as thunder. "What a huge voice I have," he thought. "Why, I could squash elephants!"

Hare jumped when he heard the fierce, echoing voice of the thing in his house. He hurried off to get some small animal friends to help.

"Who's there?" the small animal friends asked. "Who's in Hare's house?"

"Me," called Caterpillar. "I eat my way through the world. And—I can squash elephants!"

"Goodness!" The animals shivered.
"We don't want to be eaten
   through."

While Hare was wondering what to do, Fox came along.

"Fox, there's a terrible thing in my house. Could you trick
  it out with your cunning?"

"I expect so." Fox grinned. "Who's there?" Fox asked
  cleverly. "Who's in Hare's house?"

"Me," shouted Caterpillar. "I have more legs than there
  are trees in the forest. I eat my way through the world.
  And—I can squash elephants!"

Fox imagined what a terrible beast must be inside the cave. She hurried off.

"Sorry, Hare," she called. "I have to go to a chicken meeting. Why not ask Tiger? She's enormously brave."

Hare found enormously brave Tiger and brought her to the house.

"Who's there?" Tiger roared. "Who's in Hare's house?"

"Me," bawled Caterpillar. "Shaped like a rainbow, I have more legs than there are trees in the forest. I eat my way through the world. And—I can squash elephants!"

Tiger considered the size of a rainbow and pictured what the beast in Hare's house must look like.

Then she remembered she had to be enormously brave on the other side of the jungle. "Get Leopard to coax the beast out. He is very beautiful."

Leopard was admiring his spots in a pool. "Certainly I'll help." He purred.

"Who's there?" he whispered into the cave. "Who's in Hare's house?"

"Me," rumbled Caterpillar. "I knock spots off other animals."

Leopard didn't like the idea of having his spots knocked off. "You'd better go see the King," he told Hare.

King Lion was brushing his hairy mane. "Of course I shall help, dear boy," he said.

"Who is there?" Lion asked regally. "Who is in Hare's house?"

"Me." The cheeky Caterpillar preened. "I am covered with long spiky hair. Shaped like a rainbow, I have more legs than there are trees in the forest. I eat my way through the world. And—I can squash elephants!"

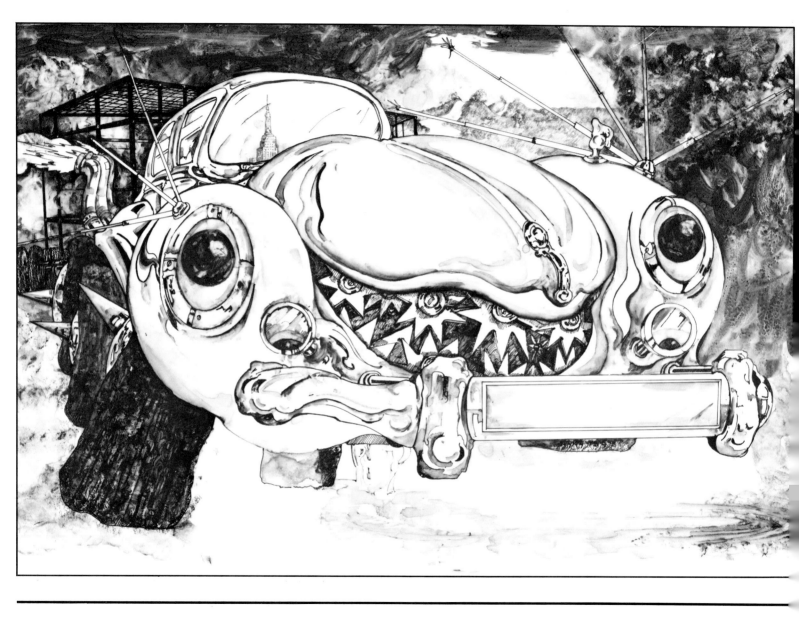

Lion thought what such a beast must look like. Then he remembered a state occasion he had to attend.

"I cannot help you, Hare. Possibly the Queen of Birds might."

Hare traveled to the mountains and found Eagle. He told her of his trouble and begged her help.

"Surely," shrilled the mighty bird.
She flew down to the jungle with
Hare.

"Who's there?" Eagle screeched. "Who's in Hare's house?"

"Me," screamed the cocky Caterpillar. "When I grow up, my wings will flatten mountains. I am covered with long spiky hair. Shaped like a rainbow, I have more legs than there are trees in the forest. I eat my way through the world. And—I can squash elephants!"

Eagle thought what such a beast must look like. "Do you fly now?" she asked.

"Er . . . no," replied Caterpillar.

"Good," Eagle said. She flew away.

"But what shall I do?" Hare called after her.

"I have a suggestion," Giraffe said slowly. "With my long neck I might peep into your cave and see what the beast really looks like. Then we can decide what to do for the best."

Giraffe quietly had a look into the cave, getting his neck into a tangle.

"Well?" Hare asked.

"It's a great dark, that's all I could see."

The animals all shivered and shook as they thought what the great dark beast must look like.

Tired and weary from his efforts, Hare decided to ask one more animal to help. The biggest and strongest in the jungle.

"Elephant?" he said.

"Hmmm," said Elephant, without moving.

"I'll help," sniffed an old frog, hopping up.

"You?" Hare laughed. "How can you help when the great
animals are helpless?"

"Well"—Frog coughed because she had a cold—"I'll try."

She hopped up to Hare's house and croaked,
"Who's there? Who's in Hare's house?"

"Me," bellowed the saucy Caterpillar. "When I grow up, my wings will flatten mountains. I am covered with long spiky hair. Shaped like a rainbow, I have more legs than there are trees in the forest. I eat my way through the world—"

The animals shivered and thought about the beast.

"When I sneeze, the earth cracks open. Cities crumble. Deserts are swept into the seas. The sky itself falls down. And— Ah . . . ah . . . ah-choo!"

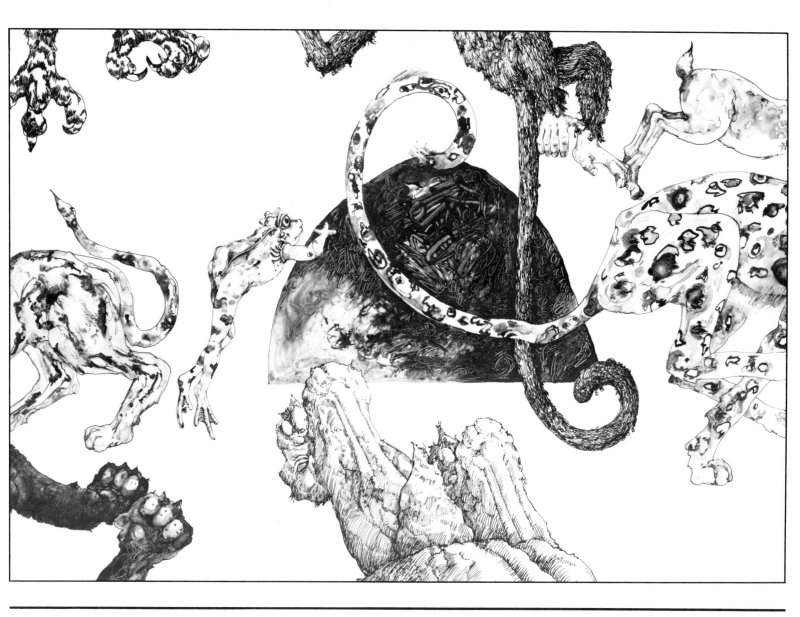

Caterpillar sneezed.

The jungle was filled with animals running away from the terrible things that would happen—all except Frog.

"Huh," she said. "You can't be much of a beast to catch my cold." She leaped into the cave and chased the cheeky Caterpillar out.

All the animals laughed when they came back and saw him, remembering what they had thought he looked like. Except Elephant, who just said, "Hmmm."

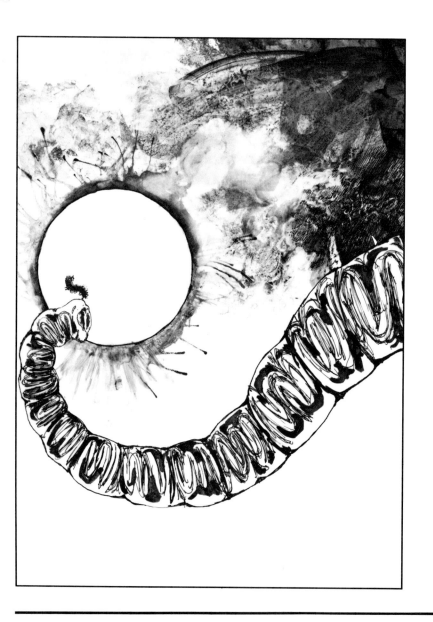

"Well, I do eat my way through the world," sniffed Caterpillar. "And I've got lots of legs and a sort of rainbow shape . . . and I can squash . . ."

DATE			
DE '91			